Raven
A Fallen Snow
Companion Novella

ABBY FARNSWORTH

World Castle Publishing, LLC
Pensacola, Florida
Copyright © 2025 Abby Farnsworth
Paperback ISBN: 9798891263734
eBook ISBN: 9798891263741
First Edition World Castle Publishing, LLC, May 19, 2025
http://www.worldcastlepublishing.com

Licensing Notes

Cover: Cover Designs by Karen
Editor: Karen Fuller

Contents

A Message to the Reader

Dear Reader, if this is the first of my books you've picked up, I want to give you a little context for what you're about to read. This novella takes place between the events of *Moonlit Skies* and *Fallen Snow*, the last two books in the EverGreen Trilogy. The main character in this story, Delilah, is, in fact, one of the primary antagonists in both of those books. As you will see throughout the story, I did not attempt to make her into a hero or even a victim. But the truth is, no one is a villain in their own story. As you read *Raven*, you will see the world through Delilah's point of view. Though I do not expect you to sympathize with her or agree with any of her actions, I do hope you will be able to enjoy learning about these events from her perspective. After all, each of us has a story to tell. As always, happy reading!

Acknowledgments

As always, thank you to Karen Fuller and World Castle Publishing for all that you do. Thank you to my loyal service dog, Zeus, for hanging out with me during the very emotional process of writing this book. And, of course, thank you to my friends, family, and everyone else who has encouraged me to continue writing. Thank you to the local business owners and non-profits who have supported my work. Lastly, thank you to my lovely readers who have been with me every step of the way.

Dedication

To the villains who could have been
heroes. Maybe in another life.

"I measure every Grief I meet
With narrow, probing, eyes –
I wonder if It weighs like Mine –
Or has an Easier size.

I wonder if They bore it long –
Or did it just begin –
I could not tell the Date of Mine –
It feels so old a pain –

I wonder if it hurts to live –
And if They have to try –
And whether – could They choose between
–
It would not be – to die –"

"I Measure Every Grief I Meet" by Emily
Dickinson

Prologue

It was after midnight, and he still hadn't come home. This wasn't acceptable. As soon as Silas walked through the front door, he was going to hear all about it. I simply would not allow him to spend so much time with that little blond-haired nuisance any longer. I'd let him toy around with her for the past several months without much complaint, but that was going to stop. I would give Silas an ultimatum. It was me or her, and I was confident he would make the right choice. And after what I was prepared to tell him tonight, there was no doubt in my mind that he would see the error of his ways.

I iced sweet tea around in my glass,

watching as the ice cubes clunked into each other. Normally, I would have been enjoying a nice glass of wine, or sipping on some fruity drink Silas had prepared for me, but tonight was different. I was done with alcohol…at least for the next nine months. My whole world was about to change.

I hadn't intentionally gotten pregnant. This wasn't some sort of scheme to convince Silas to dump her for me. Though, truthfully, the idea had occurred to me more than once. However, my general dislike for children outweighed the benefit of trapping Silas with a baby. But now that the opportunity was laid before me…well…I wasn't going to turn it down.

On a deep, primal level, I knew Silas wanted a son. He was just that type of man. I'd never had any urge to become a mother. Unlike some women, the idea of carrying a child didn't appeal to me. It seemed like a foreign concept, almost unnatural. I knew that wasn't the case. Maybe it had something to do with the fact that I'd never really known my own mother. Pregnancy wasn't something I knew much about, which was probably why it seemed so strange to me. But now I was prepared to not only embrace this new phenomenon but also use it to my advantage.

As soon as Silas discovered I was carrying his child, he would forget about his little pet entirely and give all his attention to me. It was a refreshing idea. I was done sharing him, especially with such a scrawny little weakling. Athena was pitiful, to say the least. She let Silas push her around, something I would never do. I knew how to stand up to him and had him wrapped around my finger. Silas would never have the opportunity to abuse me because I simply wouldn't let him.

I was the type of woman he needed: intelligent, insightful, and unstoppable. Not to mention my physical attributes. Athena was...colorless. Her blond hair and sickly-looking form made her seem like a walking corpse. She had lost the natural glow I remember her having years ago when we were still in school. Athena was no longer a bouncing, irresistible cheerleader. Now, she was nothing more than a twig with no sense of self-worth or confidence. It was sickening, actually. I could never imagine being so helpless.

Unlike Athena, I was vibrant. My long raven hair tumbled down around my body like waves of ebony water. Though my skin was pale, it was silky, smooth, and luminous. I had fiery red lips and piercing eyes that could intimidate even the proudest of men. There was nothing bland or uninteresting about my figure. I was stunning and fully aware of it.

Setting my tea down on the nightstand, I picked up the pregnancy test. It was as clear as it had been four hours ago with two bright blue lines. Silas could not deny that I was carrying his child, and he would have to learn to live with it.

Chapter One
LATE

As the clock struck three, Silas walked through the door. I gave him a glare that would have sent most men dashing back out the door. He stared at me with a bored expression on his face. The room was deathly quiet, almost as if even the house knew what kind of discussion was about to ensue.

"You're late," I said.

"And?" Silas replied.

"I told you that you needed to be here six hours ago. What were you doing?" I asked.

Silas rolled his eyes. "You know exactly where I was, Delilah. I'm not playing this game. I'm tired."

"Oh, you're tired?" I hissed. "How unfortunate."

He stared at me with irritation. "Let it go, or I'll leave."

I stood from my comfortable position with ease, dusting my black dress off as I stepped toward him in my stilettos. Silas let his eyes roam up and down, clearly enjoying what he was seeing. I snapped my fingers, bringing his attention back up to my face.

"You're going to sit down, and you're going to listen," I whispered.

He rolled his eyes. "Fine."

I nodded, motioning toward the velvet couch. He pulled his white dress shirt off, slumping down on the couch, wearing nothing other than a pair of black trousers. I glanced at his bare chest, admiring the view. He looked good. There was no denying it. He was my type, too: muscled, tall, and charming. Though I could have stared at him all day, I would never admit it. If he knew he had that much power over me, it wouldn't be good.

"You're going to stop seeing her," I said.

Silas raised his eyebrows. "Excuse me?"

"You heard what I said," I replied.

He scoffed. "That's not happening."

I crossed my arms over my chest. "You don't need her. I'm more than enough, and you know it. She's a plaything, and I'm tired of having her distract you."

Silas pursed his lips. "She's my girlfriend."

I raised my eyebrows. "Oh really? What am I, then? Because if she's what you really want, I'll walk away. I don't need you."

He would never let that happen.

Silas was too territorial to let a woman he wanted slip away. He was far too proud to let himself be abandoned. I contained my smirk, though. This was a game I had to play very carefully. If he didn't believe my threats, they were useless.

His eyes softened. "You know you're important to me, Delilah. There's no reason to feel so threatened. If I didn't want you, I wouldn't be here."

"If you really wanted to be here, you would have come before three in the morning, Silas," I hissed.

He shook his head. "You know I had to wait until she fell asleep."

I scowled. "Just get rid of her and be done with it," I replied.

"What exactly do you mean by that?" he asked.

I raised my eyebrows. "You know what I mean. You've done it before, Silas.

Don't pretend to be so innocent."

"We're not going to talk about this," he growled.

"Oh, we are. There's no more debate. I know your deepest, darkest secrets, Silas. There's no playing nice-boy around here," I whispered.

Silas stood, walking over to me with the strength of an angry lion about to devour his prey. I stood my ground, though. One thing I would never do was cower to a man.

"Don't give me attitude," he said.

His face was only inches away from mine, and he reached up to put his hands on my hips. With one tug, our bodies were pressed together. His heart was pounding in his chest, and I knew exactly the kind of rage I was stirring up in his ready-to-explode heart. Silas was getting angry, and I liked it. These games were more fun when there was actual risk involved.

Unlike with Athena, Silas had never raised his fists to me. I wouldn't let him. He knew that in order to keep getting what he wanted, he could not treat me the way he did other women. I didn't tolerate his drunken fits or morning fights. If he wanted to keep me around, he would be on his best behavior.

"I can speak to you however I want," I whispered, placing my hand against his chest.

Silas paused for a moment, leaning into my touch. I rubbed my thumb back and forth across his bare skin, making his breath catch more than once. He was addicted to me, and I loved it. Perhaps it was because I was different from Athena. Maybe that's why he couldn't bring himself to risk losing me. I gave him a challenge, something he'd never faced before.

He leaned down to press a kiss against

my neck. "Let's just forget about it. I hate fighting with you."

I resisted the urge to smile. He crumbled before me, and I relished in the sight of watching him fall. Silas continued kissing my neck softly, leaving gentle marks from my earlobe to my collarbone.

"I have to tell you something," I whispered in his ear.

"Oh, what's that?" he asked.

I pressed my hand harder against his chest, forcing him to look up at me. Silas gave me an irritated look but obeyed. I knew he was eager to end the conversation. In truth, so was I. This needed to be said, though.

"I'm pregnant, Silas," I whispered.

For the first time in our relationship, he did something completely unexpected. Silas stepped away from me, his eyes wide with anger and hands shaking.

"What?" he shouted.

I flinched, unable to help myself. "You heard me…I'm pregnant."

Silas stood still for a moment, seemingly unable to move. I crossed my arms over my chest, waiting for him to reply. This was not how I had pictured this conversation going. He was supposed to be happy or at least accepting.

"You're not serious," he said. "Is this a joke?"

I frowned. "No, it's the truth."

Silas threw his hands up. "Well, are you even sure it's mine?"

There was so much anger in my body that I couldn't contain myself. Before he had a chance to blink, I grabbed the closest thing to me, a glass of water, and threw it at him. The glass collided with his shoulder, cracking into a million pieces. Now wet and bleeding, Silas looked at me with furry in his eyes.

"What is wrong with you?" he shouted.

"Are you serious? Of course, the baby is yours!" I screamed.

Silas stormed toward me, grabbing my arm so hard it hurt. He glared down at me, blood dripping from where tiny pieces of glass were embedded within his skin. I tried to pull my arm away, but he only gripped it harder.

"If you ever do anything like that again, I will kill you," he whispered.

Even though I was terrified, it didn't stop me from throwing that anger right back at him. "It wouldn't be the first time you disposed of a woman's body, would it?"

I knew the truth about Silas, the things he would never tell another woman. Deep down, Silas knew I was just as bad as him. Maybe he didn't know all the things I'd tried to do, but he could sense my nature. We were both rotten to the core, completely unredeemable. That's why he trusted me with the stories of his most evil deeds. Silas knew I would never report any of it.

He'd killed at least three women I knew of, maybe more. They were all previous partners from long before Silas and I had ever met. He couldn't let women go, at least not in the traditional sense. Instead, when he got tired of a woman, he added her to his collection. There was a spot in the woods, right underneath a large magnolia tree, where their bodies lay. Every so often, he visited them and laid flowers on their unmarked graves.

The knowledge should have bothered me. In fact, if I had any sort of sense, I would have run as far away from him as possible. But I was determined to be the one woman that Silas would never tire of. Unlike the other women he discarded as broken toys, Silas would never get bored of me. I wouldn't let it happen.

"We're not talking about this," he said.

"Why not?" I replied.

Silas grabbed his shirt and slipped it over his head. I watched as he grabbed his car keys from the coffee table and began walking toward the door. He didn't even glance back at me.

"Where are you going?" I hissed.

Silas turned around, his eyes full of irritation. "None of your business."

I pursed my lips. "I'm going to be the mother of your child. Everything you do is my business, now."

He shook his head, pointing toward my stomach. "No, you're going to take care of that, and I'm never going to hear about it again."

"And if I refuse?" I asked.

Silas turned back, opened the door, and said over his shoulder. "Then I'll do it myself."

After that, the door slammed shut.

Chapter Two
ONE DARK AND STORMY NIGHT

The next morning, I lay awake in bed with a pounding headache. Silas had left last night and not returned. He was either with Athena right now or with another woman. There was no chance he'd spent the night alone. It wouldn't have bothered me so much, except I suspected that he had feelings for her. I knew he did for me, too. What I wasn't sure of was which one of us he cared for more. That was the complicated part.

Last night had not at all gone as expected. I had genuinely believed that as soon as I told Silas the news, he would drop down on his knees in front of me and vow to never be with another woman again.

Apparently, that had been a stupid idea. He was too stubborn for that. I had never imagined he would actually tell me to get rid of the baby, though.

True, I wasn't exactly enthusiastic about being a mother. I couldn't imagine myself getting up every night to feed a crying baby or change its diapers. That had never been in the plan. But now that I knew there was a little life inside me, I couldn't stop thinking about it. I didn't understand where it came from, but I felt a sense of protectiveness over this new thing I'd created. Even though I couldn't name the source of these convictions, I was determined not to do my child any harm.

I was only five weeks pregnant, barely far enough along to know. But I had taken too many tests to count. There was no doubt that I was pregnant, and Silas couldn't just make our baby disappear. I had a doctor's appointment scheduled for tomorrow that would give him yet another wake-up call about our current situation. After seeing the scan, there was no way he could avoid the truth. I was going to have this baby whether he liked it or not.

Silas would come around. He just needed a little time. Maybe it had been bad to tell him such news late at night. For all I knew, he could have been fighting with Athena before he came to see me. His moods were unpredictable, but I was usually able to keep him under control. For some reason, though, last night had been different.

I had actually considered shocking him. As a lightning faerie, that was something I could do without any real effort. Silas would have been on his knees screaming in pain if I'd so much as given him a little zap. But he didn't know I was a faerie, and I wasn't planning on telling him anytime soon. It was safer if I kept that secret to myself, especially now that I was pregnant. Our baby would likely inherit my abilities, which could put it in danger. There were certain Fae that didn't believe humans and faeries should procreate together. In fact, I'd worked with several of them before. I didn't share their belief. Yet until now, I hadn't cared one way or another if all half-faerie or demi-fae children were killed. It simply wasn't my battle to fight. But now that I was pregnant, my feelings were beginning to shift.

Not only was I unwilling to harm this child, but I wouldn't let anyone else do so, either. My mother had never protected me. It wasn't her fault, though. She had died when I was young. My child's life would be different, though. I would not let him or her go through any sort of pain. Silas was just going to have to deal with it.

I threw off my black silk covers and slid out of bed. This was not the day to lay around like a pitiful damsel in distress. I had to fight for myself because no one else would. That was the way it had always been, and I didn't expect it to change anytime soon.

I pulled my closet doors open and grabbed one of my many black dresses. This one was more…respectable than most of my other options. I had never been one for modesty. It just wasn't my thing. I didn't see any reason to cover up my physical assets, especially when I could use them to my advantage. After all, that was how I'd captured Silas.

———

I was just starting my shift at Sky's Bar and Grill when he walked in. On Monday through Saturday nights, I was the bartender there; we weren't open on Sundays. The pay wasn't great, but the men always tipped generously...especially when I was dressed to attract the male gaze. Silas walked right over to me, his eyes roaming up and down my body. I smiled at him, not wanting anything other than a nice tip and maybe some flirty conversation. He was handsome. There was no doubt about it. His smirk made me blush, which seemed to make some of the other male customers jealous. I couldn't help it, though. Silas was by far the most attractive man there. Most of my customers were older with shaggy gray beards, unkempt hair, and bad breath. Silas, on the other hand... well, he might as well have been a Greek god. There was something in his eyes that made me want to fall apart.

He looked right at me, saying, "Hello, love."

All the eyes in the room were suddenly on my body. Although there was loud music blasting, and TVs playing, everything seemed to go silent. All I could focus on was him. He knew it, too. A few of the other men shifted around in their seats. Although Silas was the youngest of my patrons, he was clearly the alpha in the room.

"How can I help you," I whispered.

He smirked. "Whisky, whatever you've got."

I nodded. "Of course."

A couple of the other men grumbled something too quietly for me to hear. Silas slid onto a bar stool, pulling a cigar out of his pocket. He shrugged his suit jacket off, laying it on top of the bar. Without trying to appear too distracted, I pulled the most expensive bottle of whisky off the top shelf. If he was going to ruffle my feathers, I'd make him pay for it.

Silas seemed to know exactly what I was doing. As soon as I set the drink down in front of him, he began swirling the glass around. He glanced down at my tight mini-skirt and low-cut top. There was nothing secretive about his *intentions.*

"I'll take another beer, hunny," one of the other men said.

I nodded. "Coming up."

As soon as I gave the other customer his drink, Silas beckoned me back over. I took a deep breath, trying not to look too flustered. He took a sip of whiskey, not once taking his eyes off of me.

"Yes?" I said.

"What's your name, love?" he asked.

I fluttered my eyelashes, giving him a smile. "Delilah."

He nodded. "Silas."

"Is there something else I can get you?" I asked.

"Actually, there is," he replied.

I watched as Silas pulled a one-hundred-dollar bill out of his pocket. My eyes grew wide, not exactly sure what he was wanting. If it was what I suspected, that was not on the table. I was a bartender, nothing more.

"Give me your number, and this is yours," he said.

I blushed, slightly embarrassed by his offer. I wasn't going to turn it down, though. Even without the payment, I would have agreed to go out with him. Silas was...intoxicating. There was no other word for the way he made my head spin.

"Okay," I whispered.

Somewhat discreetly, I pulled a pen and sticky note out of my pocket. With shaking hands, I wrote down my number. His eyes were like fire on my skin. I tried not to blush even more as he reached out to run his fingers over my arm.

"Here you go," I said.

He took the slip from me, nodding in approval. "Good."

As I started to turn away, he grabbed my hand. He placed the money in my palm and then closed my fingers around it. I raised my eyebrows.

"Buy yourself something pretty for tomorrow night," he said.

"I work tomorrow," I replied.

"When do you get off?" he asked.

I looked directly into his mesmerizing eyes. "Not until four in the morning."

He shrugged. "That's fine. I'll pick you up after work."

Normally, I would have played hard to get. But for some reason, I didn't feel the need to with Silas. I wanted him more than I could rationally explain to myself. I certainly wasn't a stranger to going out with dangerous men. It didn't trouble me at all. The difference was I usually teased them first. I enjoyed watching them squirm for weeks as I turned down their offers, all the while sending them tempting glances across the room. But with Silas, I didn't want to waste any time.

"I should get back to work," I said.

He released my hand. "I'll be here."

The rest of the night, I felt his eyes on me.

Silas didn't glance away once. Even as I smiled and laughed with other men, he didn't take his gaze off my body. I'd never met a man like that before. Though this wasn't the first place I'd served drinks, it was certainly the one with the worst reputation. All of the customers were well aware of that and took advantage of the opportunities provided to them. Silas seemed to know it, too. But unlike the other girls working at Sky's, I was insistent on never trading dates for extra cash. Though I certainly wasn't dressed modestly, all the men knew I wasn't an easy catch. I only wanted to go out with men who piqued my interest, and Silas certainly fit into that category.

As the night went on, I imagined exactly how I'd make Silas fall for me. How I'd make him beg to be mine. I knew exactly what made men like him tick, what caused them to finally open their hearts to a woman who challenged them. Silas was the type of man I wanted, and I was

the kind of woman he needed. It wouldn't take
me long to make him realize that.

————————

It wasn't hard to remember the
night I met him. In fact, that memory was
seared in the back of my mind like a brand.
Though I had thought I loved other men
before, including Rowan Marx, my former
boyfriend, Silas, was different. He made
me feel nervous, something no other man
had ever done. Some women might have
said that was the perfect reason to get as
far away from him as possible, but that
wasn't how I viewed it. In the back of my
mind, I knew I was stronger than he ever
would be. Having supernatural powers
gave me an edge, especially since he didn't
know anything about them. Silas may have
thought I was just another little woman for
him to toy around with, but that wasn't
the case. Eventually, he would discover

that it was me who actually controlled our relationship.

I slipped into my dress and grabbed a pair of black stilettos. They were leather with spikes on the heel. I planned to continue wearing these horribly uncomfortable shoes until pregnancy made my feet swell so much that I couldn't take the pain anymore. After that, I might have to take a break from bartending. Being pregnant probably wouldn't earn me the best tips. Silas would take care of me, though. He always did, at least financially.

I swept my hair back in a long, smooth ponytail that fell down to my waist. Just because Silas had been angry last night didn't mean I was going to let my appearance be anything less than perfect. He was going to regret speaking to me like that, and I'd make him plead for forgiveness.

With one last glance in the mirror, I

grabbed my purse and prepared to take on the day.

Chapter Three
WHAT WILL BABY BE

I walked into the doctor's office with a big wad of cash in my outrageously-expensive purse. As soon as I opened the door and approached the counter, the receptionist gave me a skeptical look. I knew exactly what she was thinking. All she saw was a young woman wearing a tight black dress, scandalously high heels, and a little too much eyeliner for the average person's taste. I didn't care, though. The receptionist was a tiny old woman who appeared to be in her late seventies and looked as if she had never had a day of fun in her life. It didn't matter what she thought of me.

I leaned against the white countertop.

"I'm Delilah. I have an appointment at two o'clock. Are there any papers I need to sign?"

She gave me a tight nod, handing over a clipboard. "Yes, fill these out."

I took the forms from her without a word and walked over to sit down in one of the uncomfortable plastic chairs. It wasn't a bad doctor's office, just not welcoming. That didn't bother me, though. I wasn't exactly the warm and fuzzy type. Cold, sterile equipment was fine with me. My goal was to get this done as quickly and efficiently as possible to make sure I provided Silas with a son. After that, he would be mine forever.

After I finished filling out the forms, I took them back up to the receptionist. She looked at me with annoyance, and I knew exactly why. My expression remained blank, though.

"You didn't list any insurance," she

said.

"I don't have any," I replied.

She frowned. "How will you be paying?"

I set my purse, a gift from Silas, down on the counter. "Cash."

She watched in annoyance as I handed her a stack of fifty-dollar bills. "I see. Today's visit will be two hundred. Is that alright with you?"

"Yes," I replied. "I always want to go ahead and pay for whatever test it is that confirms the baby's gender."

"How far along are you?" she asked.

"Five weeks," I replied.

She began counting the cash. "We can't do that test yet. You need to be at least another month along before we can tell if the baby is a boy or a girl."

I frowned. "Okay, then I'd like to schedule another appointment four weeks from now."

She looked at me skeptically. "You don't want to talk to the doctor first?"

I shook my head. "No."

The receptionist shrugged and handed me my change. "It's your money. Four weeks from today, then?"

"That's fine," I replied.

Just a few moments later, a nurse called my name. Before I turned to walk through the now-open door, I saw the receptionist roll her eyes. It took all of my self-control not to turn around and show her exactly what it felt like to have lighting running through your bones. I didn't need to expose myself like that, though, at least not here.

The nurse led me to a small white room with two chairs and an examination chair. I sat down, crossing my legs one over the other. She opened her laptop and began asking me questions. I answered them mindlessly without trying to appear too disinterested. Though I didn't really care about my own health, I did want to make sure the baby was okay. Silas wouldn't want a sick son. I had to give him a healthy child in order for this plan to work. Otherwise, he wouldn't view it as worth his time to stick around.

"I see you're very eager to learn the gender," she said.

I nodded. "Yes, but I was told I have to wait for that."

She smiled. "I understand. It's hard not knowing. I was so excited when I had my first baby. My husband was really hoping for a girl, and luckily enough, that's exactly what we got."

The nurse looked like a nice girl. She was probably in her mid-twenties with light brown hair, crystal-blue eyes, and plump pink lips. I wouldn't have called her stunning, but she was probably more attractive than most women I knew.

When I didn't reply, the nurse just glanced back down at her laptop. "Well, I'll send the doctor in."

She left the room in a hurry, seemingly eager to escape my presence. It wasn't that I hated other women. In fact, some of them seemed interesting and pleasant. But I didn't feel the need to be friends with any of them, either. I didn't crave relationships in general. Most of the time, I was perfectly happy on my own. It didn't matter to me when the other girls from work would all go out together, and I wasn't invited. I knew my presence would only cause them to feel awkward. Making friends wasn't something I'd ever wanted, no less been good at.

With men, though, it was a little different. I liked their attention. Maybe it was because I had some internalized fear that I wasn't adequate, or perhaps I just wanted to be praised. Either way, I enjoyed the way most of them seemed to hand me their hearts without a second thought. If nothing else, having them beg me for acknowledgement kept life from getting too dull.

I had once wondered if I was a narcissist. If that was the truth, it would certainly explain a lot about me. Most of the time, I didn't care if others lived or died, but that wasn't always the case. When it came to this new baby, all of the rules I had once thought applied to me seemed to melt away. Not only did I want this child to be healthy for Silas, but also because it was important to me. I'd never cared about another living being the way I did about this little life developing inside my body. I wanted the baby to be...happy. Not just content or satisfied, but happy. It was strange to care so much about the feelings of another creature, and I wasn't sure what to do about it. In a way, having such hopes made me feel vulnerable.

The door opened, and a middle-aged man stepped in. My eyes grew wide as I recognized him from work. Ivan was one of my regular customers, but I'd never known what he did for work. We didn't spend much time talking about occupations. He wasn't ugly, but he certainly wasn't handsome, either. I didn't mind, though. His tips over the past two weeks had more than paid for this appointment. That was enough to make me talk to him whenever he sat down and asked for a drink. He gave me a smirk, closing the door behind him.

"Well, Miss Delilah, it's nice to see you," he said.

I gave him a tight smile. "You, too. I

didn't realize this was your office. In fact, I didn't know you were a doctor."

He grinned. "We learn things every day."

I folded my hands in my lap, waiting for him to speak again. This wasn't meant to be a small talk session. I was here to learn about the baby, and that was all. It wasn't just another night at the bar when I'd flirt with him, and he'd give me a generous tip.

"I will say, I didn't expect to see you here," he said.

I shrugged. "Looks like we're both surprised."

He nodded. "Indeed. If I may ask, who is the father?"

"Is it a medical question or a personal one?" I asked.

Ivan sat down across from me. "Both."

I rolled my eyes. "You know who it is."

He crossed his arms over his chest. "Silas? I didn't think you two were that serious. Is your relationship with him going somewhere?"

"That's none of your business," I replied.

Ivan shrugged. "Well, if I was the father, I'd take better care of you than he's going to."

I laughed, not able to stop myself before the noise came out of my mouth. "That's ridiculous. You're married, Ivan."

"And?" he asked. "That doesn't mean I wouldn't provide for you and the baby. I can certainly afford it."

"Your wife might not like that," I replied.

He smiled. "I keep her content with unlimited spending money. She doesn't involve herself in my business, and I don't pry too closely into hers."

I shrugged. "That's one way to do it."

Ivan leaned back. "But Silas, well, he's not known for his reliability. At least according to all the rumors I've heard."

I froze. "And what might those be?"

Ivan smirked. "Do you really want to know, Delilah?"

I never let men believe they had the upper hand. The fact that Ivan had the information I wanted made me furious. This wasn't how it was supposed to go. Somehow, I needed to get it out of him without seeming weak or desperate. The last thing I wanted was for him to think I was here begging for help.

I laced my fingers together. "If you're in the mood to tell me."

Ivan laughed. "Ever the temptress. Well, he's been toying around with some blond for a long while now. Rumor has it they even live together. Doesn't seem like something you'd be okay with, at least not if you're the woman I think you are."

"What does that mean?" I hissed.

He shrugged. "You deserve better than that, Delilah."

I frowned. "You seem to be implying something."

He nodded. "It's not right for you to let him treat you like trash. I may not be able to move in with you, but at least I wouldn't be living my life with another woman behind your back. I'd give you everything you could ever want, including a home for that baby."

"Why would you do that?" I asked.

Ivan laughed. "I'd love to have you all to myself. For that luxury, there's not a price I wouldn't pay."

I leaned forward. "So you mean to say that you'd like me to be your mistress?"

He nodded. "Precisely."

I stood, a scowl on my face. "This conversation is over. I'm perfectly happy right where I am. And for the record, my personal life is none of your business."

"Delilah, wait," he said, "don't be upset."

"Do not tell me what to do," I hissed.

He reached into his pocket and pulled out two one-hundred-dollar bills. "Look, just keep the money. It's not like I wouldn't have given it back to you eventually, anyway."

I resisted the urge to slap him. "I don't want charity."

Ivan rolled his eyes. "That's not what this is. Look, I'll order your blood work. Just think about my offer and come back in a month."

Without another word, I walked out of the room and slammed the door behind me.

Chapter Four
SATISFACTORY

We had been seated by the restaurant nearly five minutes ago, and neither of us had spoken a single word since. Silas was sipping his Bourbon while I swirled the water around in my glass. It wasn't the most awkward silence we'd ever experienced, but there was certainly tension. I didn't want to be the first one to speak, so he would have to give in, or we'd spend our whole meal in silence.

"How was your day?" he asked.

The words slid out of his mouth like needles ready to pierce my skin. Silas clearly wasn't in the mood for a full-blown argument. That was good news, at least for me. Maybe we could carefully avoid the events of last night and still have a pleasant meal. Until I learned the baby's gender, I didn't plan on discussing the pregnancy with him again.

"It was fine, yours?" I asked.

He nodded. "Busy. Work has been chaotic lately."

I knew Silas worked in finance, but that was about it. He never spoke much about work or his life outside of me. Our conversations were limited in scope, but I didn't mind. We each liked a bit of privacy. I wasn't so controlling that I wouldn't let him have his secrets. Yet when it came to him seeing other women, well, that would have to end.

"And…Athena?" I asked.

Silas rolled his eyes. "Now is not the time to bring her up. Just pick something else to talk about, Delilah. I'm not in the mood."

I took a sip of water. "Neither am I."

He was restraining himself. That much was clear. We were in the middle of a crowded restaurant. It wasn't necessarily fancy, but the place wasn't a dump, either. It was classy enough that I'd put on a new dress. It was the type Silas liked: thin and barely-there. The red fabric hugged all of my curves, showing off the more plentiful parts of my body. And while some women may have felt insecure wearing such a tight dress, it gave me a sense of power. I was confident and proud of my figure, which was much more than most people could say.

The waiter came up to our table and asked what we wanted to eat. Silas ordered for both of us, something he liked to do. I allowed him those small pleasures, the ones that made him believe he was still in control. Of course, that was about as far from the truth as possible. Every ounce of power he had in this relationship was granted to him by me. The amusing thing was he had no clue that he wasn't in control.

I enjoyed our little game, though. It was what kept things interesting. But in truth, I held all the cards. But like an expert playing with a novice, I sometimes let him win. It allowed him to maintain his fragile ego and not feel like a total pushover.

"The pasta sounds perfect, good choice," I said.

He smiled in satisfaction. "I knew you'd like it."

I had to prevent myself from laughing. It didn't matter to me whether he ordered spaghetti, salmon, or anything else on the menu. But the fact that he felt so accomplished and proud, well, that was the best part of all.

"Are you hungry?" I asked.

He nodded. "Very."

Silas had an amazing body. There was no doubt about it. He was tall, muscled, and had a sort of bad-boy style that I loved. His hair was full and lustrous, and his eyes held the perfect mixture of masculinity and determination. But he loved his food, that was for sure. Having a full, satisfying meal always put him in a good mood, which was advantageous for me. It was best to keep him content; that made my task of convincing him to do whatever I wanted much easier.

"I'm sure you had a long day at work," I said.

He nodded. "Extremely busy."

"Well, you're a hard worker," I replied.

Flattering Silas was another way to put him in a good mood. He liked being complimented and fussed over. Even if all I did was give him a little praise, it was enough.

He glanced down at my neck, eyeing the gold choker and diamond charm that dangled above my collarbone. A grin crept over his face. The day he'd gifted me the necklace was still fresh in my mind. I remembered the details as clearly as if they had been yesterday.

———

I was stuck late at work, waiting for a group of men to leave before I could wipe down the counters and go home. It was already after three in the morning, and I knew Silas was waiting for me outside. He hated it when I was late, but I couldn't just kick the customers out. If I did, they definitely wouldn't give me a tip.

"Hey, how about another round?" one of them asked.

I resisted the urge to roll my eyes. "Don't you think you might want to head home? It's a weeknight. You won't get much sleep before work tomorrow."

These three were repeat customers, but I had never learned their names. They came in often enough for me to recognize them but not so much that we were well acquainted. They usually tipped well, though, so I tried to keep them satisfied.

"Nah, we've got the day off," another said.

I held in a sigh. "What will it be this time?"

"Maybe something a little more exclusive?" the first one said.

He wasn't an ugly man, but he was definitely far too old for my taste. With his salt-and-pepper beard, graying hair, and smug smile, I guessed he was in his late forties. Not old by any means, but more than double my age. Still, that didn't stop most of the men in here from flirting with the employees, who were all under thirty. A majority of the male customers didn't want anything more than a pretty face to talk to and a few smiles, but like always, there were some that wanted a special kind of attention. And a few of them had a particularly hard time taking no for an answer, especially when some of my coworkers were more than happy to oblige.

I didn't blame the other girls. Some of them had actually found love here and started meaningful relationships. One previous employee, about five years older than me, had actually met her husband here. They now had a child together and were happily married. Of course, this is also where Silas and I had met for the first time. There was always a chance of meeting the right man, but the majority of the time, that wasn't the case.

"Some of our more expensive varieties?" I asked.

He laughed. "Not necessarily. Unless you're on that list, darling. In that case, I'd definitely be interested."

His friends grinned, turning toward me

with a predatory smile. I wasn't afraid of them. If the worst happened, I'd just electrocute all three of them. That wasn't what I wanted to do, though. It would not only expose me, but I'd also probably lose my job.

Before I had the chance to respond, the front door swung open. I held in a sigh of relief as Silas strolled in. He was wearing a pair of black pants, a white dress shirt, and an outrageously expensive watch on his wrist. Silas gave me a glance of annoyance, but then his attention shifted to the men on the other side of the room.

"You three do realize this place closed a half-hour ago," he said.

The one with the salt-and-pepper beard leaned back in his chair. "We're still finishing up. If I'm lucky, I might be able to get the bartender's number before heading home."

I didn't even have the chance to blink before Silas was on the other side of the room, his fist colliding with the man's face. My jaw dropped as Silas pummeled the man into the ground. As soon as they realized what was going on, his friends jumped into action. An instant later, Silas had thrown both men to the ground. It was rare that something genuinely surprised me, but this was a rare situation. I stared at the bloody scene before me, completely confused as to what I should say or do next. Silas knelt down before all three men, a look of pure fury on his face.

"She's mine," he growled, "and if you ever so much as glance at her again, you won't live to see another day."

A moment later, he was at my side, pulling me into the night air. I let him lead me, my head still spinning with shock. Silas looked down at me, blood splattered all over his shirt.

"You never talk to them again, understood?" he asked.

I nodded. "Yes."

"Good," he replied, grabbing my wrist

and leading me toward his car.

Before he opened the door to let me in the passenger seat, he pulled something out of his pocket. I was still too confused to completely process what was going on.

"Turn around," he said.

I obeyed, not in the mood to refuse him. It was the first time I'd ever seen Silas be violent with anyone. His eyes were still glazed with anger, and his hands were red with the blood of all three men. I bit my lip, trying to calm my mind. Silas brushed my hair off my shoulders and reached around to place a gold chain around my neck. Dangling from the middle was a large, heart-shaped diamond.

"You'll wear this every day from now on," he ordered. "That way, every loser who walks in there will know you're mine."

I nodded. "Okay."

He smiled down at me. "Good."

———

Halfway through our meal, Silas glanced across the table. "I love it when you wear that necklace."

I blushed. "I'm glad."

A glimmer of satisfaction showed in his eyes. "Yes, it's quite...pleasurable."

"Well, I'm happy if you're happy," I replied.

He smiled. "As you should be."

Chapter Five
VULNERABILITY

Pregnancy was starting to affect me. I woke up in the middle of the night with terrible nausea and vomiting all over my bed. It took me a few minutes, but I was eventually able to get myself moving and put the sheets in the washer. After that, I took my silk pajamas off and stepped into the shower. The hot water helped wash some of the sickness away.

I hated feeling so helpless. Unlike most things in life, the way pregnancy impacted my body wasn't something I could control. Thankfully, Silas hadn't been there to witness the mess. It had been two weeks since our fight when I told him about the baby. He hadn't mentioned it since. I presumed he thought I had already solved the issue. That wasn't the case, though. I was determined to have this child. After the birth, I would convince him to marry me.

Silas might not have realized he wanted a son, but after he saw the baby, he would change his mind. There was no way he'd abandon his child. Silas wasn't a good person, and neither was I. Even so, leaving your own flesh and blood to fend for themselves was a different level of wrong. As much as I knew I wouldn't be a perfect mother, I wasn't going to leave this baby helpless. After all, it carried fifty percent of my DNA. If I wouldn't let myself suffer, then I couldn't let this child go through pain, either.

I washed my raven black hair, carefully separating the strands with my fingers before lathering the rest of my body with soap that smelled of peppermints and pine. The scent reminded me of Silas, and for some reason, I found it comforting. He was the only person whose presence made me relax. Apart from him, I enjoyed my solitude. But when Silas was around, my body seemed to calm in a way that it never had before.

To be honest, I wasn't sure if I believed in love. When I was younger, I'd imagined that the kind of adoration written about in fairytales was real. But over the years, I'd come to suspect that all romantic feelings were caused by simple chemical reactions. That wasn't a particularly satisfying hypothesis, though. Part of me wanted to believe that soulmates were real and all her childhood ideas about love were true. And being with Silas…it made me question everything.

I wasn't delusional enough to think

that he was completely in love with me. If that were the case, he would have stopped seeing Athena long ago. That didn't mean he felt nothing for me, though. I'd once been told that it was possible to love more than one person at the same time. Maybe that was true. If so, it certainly made everything more complicated.

When the hot water started to make me feel lightheaded, I stepped out of the shower. I dried myself with a fluffy towel, then gazed at my body in the mirror. It was too early for my stomach to grow. Yet I placed my hand over my abdomen, imagining what it would look like in a few months. Would Silas stand behind me and cradle my stomach? Would he kiss my cheek and whisper about how excited he was to hold the child inside me? What would it be like when I gave birth with him beside me, when I let my body be torn to produce the child that would provide me with exactly what I wanted? I could hardly wait to find out.

"Can you hear me in there?" I whispered.

Of course, there was no response. It was too early for the baby to kick. I had no clue if he would hear me or if he was even aware of his own existence. Perhaps the child inside me knew nothing other than warmth and safety. A warm feeling spread through my chest. For some reason, the thought made me smile. It scared me more than I cared to admit. If I learned to truly love this child, it would make me more vulnerable than ever before. I would become weak. The idea infuriated me. Maybe this was the real reason I had never wanted children.

I looked down to where my hands cradled my stomach. "What do you think about all of this? Are you…happy?"

The only answer I received was silence.

Chapter Six
BEATING HEARTS

I was just pulling the baked potatoes out of the oven when I heard the door to my apartment unlock. Silas was the only other person with a key. My apartment certainly wasn't fancy, but there wasn't anything wrong with it. I didn't need or want a huge place when I was here by myself most of the time.

There were four rooms: a kitchen, living area, bedroom, and bathroom. They were all painted a simple white with minimal black furniture. The few decorations I did have were pieces of art in different shades of red hanging from several of the walls. It was a clean, basic style, exactly what I wanted.

There was enough variety in my wardrobe that I didn't need an extravagant home. My apartment, which Silas had once said looked like no one lived in it, was enough for me.

From his few mentions of her, I knew Athena was more of a homemaker. She liked decorating, baking, and making her shared space with Silas feel comforting. That wasn't me, though. However, when I had the baby, I assumed some things would change. After all, I would need somewhere for him to sleep, as well as a place to put all of the other baby-related items. In truth, I had no idea what purchases I would need to make. It couldn't be too hard to figure out, though. I wasn't stupid, and having a baby was not exactly rocket science.

"Delilah?" Silas called.

"I'm in the kitchen," I replied.

He strolled on in, looking pristine in his black suit and navy tie. Silas leaned against the doorframe in a more relaxed way than usual. I could already tell he was in a good mood. Silas smiled at me, extending his hand toward mine. I leaned in against his chest, resting my head on his body. He wrapped his arms around me, gently running his hands up and down my back. His cologne was familiar and comforting, making my body relax as he squeezed me tighter. These moments of gentleness were rare, which caused me to enjoy each of them with a special appreciation.

Silas reached toward my chin to tilt it up and placed a soft kiss against my lips. I smiled, pressing closer to him. He reacted positively, reaching down to grip my hips as he deepened our kiss. The sweetness of his touch was enough to make me forget about everything else that had been on my mind. It was nice to let everything go for just a few moments and take pleasure in the way he made my heart beat just a little bit faster.

"You're in a good mood today," I whispered.

He chuckled. "I missed you."

A smile spread across my lips. "Oh really? How so?"

He grinned. "Work was dull, and for some reason, I kept finding myself distracted by the thought of your lips on mine."

I savored the days when his sweet words and thoughtful touches made me feel lightheaded and giddy. Of course, I would never reveal how much his affection meant to me. In truth, it would have been a monumental loss if he decided he never wanted to see me again. Silas was an important part of my life. I refused to let him go, even if that meant having to do certain things that even I knew weren't moral. He would be mine, no matter what it took.

If Athena hadn't been distracting

Silas, I never would have given her a single thought. As a person, I had nothing against her. She was probably just like every other girl who had peaked in high school and now didn't know what to do with her life. But because she loved the man I wanted to spend my life with, I hated her. Athena was an obstacle, nothing more. I would do whatever it took to get rid of her. Of course, it would have been best if Silas dumped her altogether. If that were the case, I wouldn't have to take any action at all.

The baby inside me was my best chance at convincing Silas that I was the love of his life, not her. And even if I never wanted to say those words back to him, I wanted to hear them said to me. Every woman, even those who appeared heartless, had the desire to be adored. Maybe over time, it would soften me a bit.

I leaned in closer to Silas, enjoying the

way his chest felt against my cheek. Unlike most days, I wasn't wearing a full face of makeup, and I didn't have my hair done. It was my one free night of the week. And luckily, I was spending it with him. Silas looked down into my eyes, his hand gently reaching up to tangle itself in my hair.

"Delilah...I..." he whispered.

My eyes grew wide. "Yes?"

He looked hesitant. "There's something I need to say."

My heart began beating as fast as a racehorse. "What is it?"

Silas leaned down, his lips just inches from mine. "I think I might...love you."

And at that, I was lost for words. Silas grabbed me and lifted my body up into his arms. He wrapped my legs around his waist and carried me out into the living room, where he placed me softly on the couch. I knew he could see the emotion in my eyes, and for once, I was okay with it. For just a moment, I'd let him see how much he meant to me. And though I might never say those words, he would know that buried deep in the depths of my heart, I felt exactly the same way.

"Please just…never leave," he whispered.

I pulled Silas down beside me, wrapping my arms around his neck as I kissed his cheek. He ran his hands along my back, gently massaging my skin with his steady fingers. After a few moments, he pulled me into his lap. I sighed against his lips, peppering small, quick kisses all over his face. Silas wrapped his arms tighter around me, enjoying the feel of our hearts beating against each other. For a moment, I imagined this was what true, unfiltered love was like.

"I won't, Silas," I breathed against his

lips, "I won't."

Silas tugged me against him so hard it hurt. "I need you forever."

"Yes," I whispered, "forever."

Chapter Seven
DECISIONS, DECISIONS

It was just after two in the morning when Ivan walked into Sky's Bar and Grill. My eyes grew wide as he walked over and sat directly in front of me at the bar. It was the first time we'd seen each other since my appointment. I had honestly thought that due to the strange nature of our last conversation, Ivan would never come to Sky's again. But just one night before I was supposed to be back at his office for bloodwork, he'd decided to confront me again.

I decided to pretend everything was normal. "Hello, what can I get you?"

Ivan gave me a knowing look. "I think

you know the answer to that, dear. After all, I've been a regular since before you started working here."

It was true. Prior to the last several weeks, Ivan had visited Sky's every few days. He always came alone, though. Sometimes, he would chat with other customers, but never anything other than small talk. Ivan was comfortable being alone in the midst of excitement...just like me.

I handed him his mojito. He was the only customer who ever requested it, but considering how often he typically frequented the establishment, we tried to keep the ingredients on hand. Ivan smiled at me, nodding his head in appreciation.

"Looks delicious, as always," he said.

I gave him a tight smile before walking away. For the next half-hour, Ivan watched me with passive interest. It was a Friday night, so we were extremely busy.

Customers came and went, usually only staying for one or two drinks. Finally, it was only fifteen minutes until closing, and Ivan was the only customer left.

He sat there slowly sipping his drink as I cleaned the counters. I wanted to roll my eyes, but that wouldn't help speed the process along. It was hard to tell if he was here to annoy me or to make a point, maybe both. After a while, I got sick of it.

"Are you leaving?" I hissed.

He raised his eyebrows. "Don't be so feisty. I'm just enjoying my drink."

"You've been doing that for almost an hour," I said.

He shrugged. "It's scrumptious, I'm just enjoying it."

I put my hands on my hips. "I don't know why you're here, but I'm tired. I want to go home and go to bed."

He shook his head. "Oh, sweet Delilah.

See, if you would just take me up on my offer, you wouldn't have to work at all. I'd take care of you. Wouldn't it be nice to have extra sleep in your delicate condition?"

I leaned against the counter, a sharp look in my eyes. "Nothing about me is delicate."

Ivan shrugged. "Maybe that's because you've never felt safe enough to let go."

For some reason, hearing him speak those words struck a chord within me. I never wanted anyone to view me as a wounded animal, especially not a man like Ivan. He wanted to save me like some sort of hero, but that would never happen. I didn't need to be rescued, particularly not by a man more than twice my age who wanted to turn me into his dirty little secret. Ivan may not have realized it, but what he was offering didn't appeal to me in the least. That wasn't what I wanted in life, especially when I'd already found the man I hoped to spend forever with.

"You don't know anything about me," I hissed.

Ivan took another sip of his drink. "Maybe not, but I do know something about your boyfriend. Is he really giving you more than I can offer? Think about it. It's Friday night, and who is here with you? Me, not him. Where is he, Delilah? What is he doing? I have several theories, but I doubt you want to hear them. Tell me, does he know you're pregnant?"

I slammed my hand down on the counter. "That is none of your business."

"There's a lot for you to think about, dear," he whispered. "So many decisions to be made, and at the moment, you're forced to handle them alone. Do you think a young woman like you should really be made to handle so much responsibility? I don't."

I stared directly at him, hoping my words cut like knives. "You have a daughter my age, and I doubt she'd want to hear you say those words to her."

He shrugged. "Luckily for me, she's married to a very capable young man with everything he needs to care for her. Are you in that same position? Doesn't look like it."

Unable to control myself, I grabbed a knife from under the counter. Ivan's eyes grew wide as I pointed it at him. My hands were shaking, making it almost impossible to prevent myself from doing more than just aiming the knife in his direction.

"Get out," I hissed.

Ivan slowly stood, raising his hands in the air. "Calm down, Delilah. There's no need for violence. I'm trying to help you."

"I don't care!" I shouted. "Get out!"

With fear in his eyes, Ivan slowly backed away from me until he reached the front door. As soon as the door clicked shut behind him, I let the knife fall down onto the countertop. My heart was beating quickly, but I couldn't tell whether it was from anger or anxiety. Ivan's words rang through my mind.

It was true; Silas wasn't being much help, and I didn't have anyone else. My father had abandoned me years ago, and I hadn't heard from him since. Everyone I'd ever known wanted nothing to do with me. In truth, it was my fault. In fits of uncontrollable anger, I had done monstrous things to others. Those actions had alienated me from my community, and now there was no chance of ever going back. I knew I was a bad person and that I didn't deserve anyone's pity or care, but that didn't mean being alone wasn't scary. Most of the time, I was happy with my solitude. But with a baby on the way, I was beginning to question if I continue to do things alone.

Silas would step up, though. Or at least I hoped so. And if he didn't, well, I couldn't blame him. Just like me, Silas was a bad person. We deserved each other. Perhaps that was why I wanted to hold onto him so tightly. We both had no chance of redemption. But Athena, she was good. I didn't know much about her, but from what Silas said, I could tell that she had a loving heart. She didn't deserve to be trapped with him for the rest of her life. Of course, I would never say those words out loud. Just because I knew she was good didn't mean that I cared about her. If Athena died tomorrow, I wouldn't shed any tears. But deep down, I knew she deserved better. Of course, it wasn't my fault she refused to stand up for herself. If she continued to let Silas push her around, then I refused to feel any pity for her situation.

I was different, though. Unlike Athena, I knew how to mold Silas into the man I needed him to be. Although he didn't realize it, Silas was pliable to my desires. I could make him do exactly what I wanted, all the while making him believe it was actually his idea. And truthfully, I didn't feel the least bit bad about it. Silas wasn't pure, he had also done unforgivable things, so I would never have any remorse about manipulating him. He was lucky that I even bothered to give him my attention. Though I wasn't a good person, I was beautiful. And for a man like him, that was really all that mattered.

Chapter Eight
BLOOD AND TEARS

The next morning, I marched straight into the doctor's office without any hesitation. Luckily, Ivan had stayed home due to illness, or so he said. The other patients gave me disgusted looks as I walked through the waiting room in my knee-high stiletto boots, sheer tights, leather miniskirt, and red fishnet top. Some of the surrounding women gawked at me, but I just walked right past. The nurse carefully avoided my gaze as she led me back to the same waiting room as before. I sat down in the cold, metal chair, crossing my legs and tossing my long hair over my shoulder. I didn't mind playing this part, especially when it made people afraid of me. Being feared was the easiest way to get what I wanted.

"You're here for your bloodwork?" the nurse asked.

I nodded, staring down at my long, sharp, silver nails. "Yes."

She gave me a nervous smile. "Okay, we'll take the sample here."

She left the room to collect her supplies but came back within just a few moments. Needles didn't scare me. In fact, neither did blood. There weren't many parts of life that made my stomach churn. A little blood work certainly wasn't one of them.

"Would you please hold out your arm?" she asked.

I nodded, sticking it out in her direction. She cleaned my skin with alcohol before stabbing me with the needle. I stared down as the blood began to flow. It was almost the same color as my shirt.

"So, have you thought about names?" she asked.

I raised my eyebrows. Picking a name for the child hadn't even crossed my mind. It didn't really matter to me what we called it as long as it was a boy. Maybe I'd let Silas pick the name; that would make him happy.

"No, I haven't," I replied.

She shrugged. "You have plenty of time."

There was kindness in her voice, more so than I would have expected from a stranger. She certainly suspected this was an unplanned pregnancy, which was the truth. I didn't look like the type of woman who would want to be a mother.

The nurse seemed to read my mind. "You know, when a baby is born, your maternal instincts just seem to kick in. It's natural. After that, it'll all feel like it was meant to be."

I looked away, not having a sufficient reply that would sound anything other than robotic. The nurse knew nothing about me. Most women might have had a maternal instinct, but I certainly didn't. No matter how many children I had, and I hoped it would just be one, nothing about my mind or heart would change.

After having collected several vials of blood, she pulled the needle away. "Well, you're all good to go. You should have your results in about a week."

I nodded. "Thank you."

She smiled at me. "You're welcome, Delilah."

Later that night, I was halfway through eating a box of pizza when Silas walked through the door. He looked at me with an amused expression on his face. I had my feet propped up on the coffee table, my hair tied up in a bun, and I only wore a silk robe.

Silas laughed, leaning back against the wall.

"What are you doing?" he asked.

I shrugged, taking another bite of cheese pizza. "What does it look like?"

"Any left for me?" he inquired.

I opened the box, revealing five more pieces. "Have at it."

He sat down on the couch beside me before grabbing a slice. "Well, it seems like I've missed a very enjoyable evening."

I motioned toward the TV where The Vampire Diaries was playing. "I've been entertained."

He laughed. "I can tell."

I leaned against his chest, enjoying the feel of his soft button-up against my cheek. Silas propped his head against mine, placing a small kiss on my hair. I closed my eyes, enjoying the touch.

"So, what did you do today?" he asked.

I closed my eyes, debating whether I should tell him the truth. "I had a doctor's appointment."

He looked down at me. "Are you alright?"

I nodded. "Yes."

He tilted his head to the side. "Then why did you go to the doctor?"

My heart began to beat a bit faster. "You know why, Silas."

Silas tensed. "I hope you're not implying what I suspect, Delilah. You know that won't make me happy."

"Don't overreact, Silas," I whispered.

He growled at me. "You completely ignored my instructions. I told you what to do, and you did the opposite."

I looked into his eyes. "It's my choice. You don't get to decide this for me."

His voice grew dangerously quiet. "You need to rethink those words."

"They're true," I whispered.

Silas closed his eyes, seemingly trying to control himself. "Delilah, this conversation is over."

I shook my head. "No, it's not. I'm having this baby."

He grabbed my arm so hard it hurt. "Listen to me, Delilah. This is not up for debate."

"You're right," I hissed, "it's not."

Before I had the chance to look away, Silas reached out and backhanded me across the face. My lip split open, and a trickle of blood dripped down my chin. I looked up at him in shock, completely stunned.

Silas stared at me, not an ounce of remorse in his face. "Understood?"

Blood continued to drip from my mouth, and my face was beginning to sting. My eyes were starting to water, and I looked away in an attempt to hide the tears that were desperate to fall. I would not let him see me cry, especially when I was already humiliated. With a shaking hand, I reached up to wipe the blood away. Silas leaned back against the couch as if nothing had happened.

He had never hit me before, and I'd honestly believed he never would. I was aware that he treated Athena like trash, beating her black and blue every day. But that was because she never had the nerve to oppose him. He knew he could get away with treating her like that. I was different, or at least I thought so. But what was I going to do? How would I show him that this was unacceptable? I was already on the verge of tears, and if I spoke, I knew my voice would sound weak.

"I'll take your silence as acceptance," he said.

Silas slowly reached down, turning

my face toward his. I kept my eyes closed, refusing to let him see even a hint of pain. He lifted his fingers, gently rubbing them across my lips.

"Such a shame," he whispered, "it might take days to heal." He tilted my head up, pressing his lips to mine. "Doesn't bother me, though."

I turned away, still too pained to offer a reply. He leaned forward to grab another piece of pizza. No matter how hard I tried, I couldn't seem to slow my pounding heart. A solitary tear slid down my cheek, but I reached up swiftly to wipe it away.

"And Delilah," he whispered, "if I find out that you've refused to cooperate, I'll be forced to take matters into my own hands."

Chapter Nine
TROUBLE TYPE

"Hey, what happened to your face?" Coral asked.

She was perhaps four or so years older than me, with bright blond hair, large green eyes, and creamy white skin. Coral had worked at Sky's far longer than me and was an incredibly experienced waitress. She knew how to balance stacks upon stacks of plates and drinks atop each other and was able to collect generous tips. It was no wonder that the men practically threw money at her. Coral was curvy in all the right places and knew exactly how to highlight her best features. I wasn't envious of her, though, because I knew I was just as pretty, if not more so.

"Nothing," I replied, turning away to hide my split lip from view.

I'd put dark lipstick on in an effort to distract from the injury, but it hadn't worked. Unfortunately, it was glaringly obvious to everyone that I'd been hit. No amount of makeup could distract from the swelling. I would have tried to claim it was an allergic reaction, but there wasn't enough concealer in my collection to hide the purplish hue spread across my cheek.

"Delilah, are you alright?" she asked.

I knew Coral was trying to be nice. From everything I'd witnessed, she was a sweet girl. Coral was soft and gentle, the complete opposite of me. She had a purity about her that I could only ever imagine. Maybe that was why so many of the customers specifically requested her to take their orders.

I gave her an annoyed look. "Drop it, Coral."

She looked slightly wounded at my tone. "Fine. But if you need anything, you can just ask. I can help you, or at least try."

I shook my head. "Seriously, it's nothing."

Coral turned away. "Okay, Delilah."

She was just trying to help. That much was clear. Others had given me weird looks tonight, too. I never came to work looking anything less than perfect. For what seemed like the first time in my life, I felt a bit insecure.

"I'll have another beer," a man said from behind me.

I was busy cleaning the counter off, so he startled me a bit. After what had happened with Silas, I was feeling a little jumpy. Every loud sound, unexpected movement, or strange noise made me flinch. It made me feel weak. The one positive result from all of this was that it made me entirely determined not to do what Silas wanted. I would not let him push me around like he did with every other woman. Silas was going to learn that I made my own decisions, and he did not get to decide everything for me.

I spun around, taking in the man's way black hair, clean-shaven face, and deep brown eyes. He stared at me as if he could read my mind. My own eyes grew wide as I took in his tall, lean figure, broad shoulders, and casual stance. His shirt was skin-tight, revealing a firm chest and muscled abdomen. He seemed to notice I was staring, causing a wide grin to spread across his face. I took a step back, trying to clear my mind.

"Sure," I replied.

"Thanks, gorgeous," he whispered with ease.

The man slid onto a bar stool, thanking

me as I handed him a beer. "What's your name?"

I brushed my hair off my shoulder. "Delilah."

He smiled, letting his eyes travel down my body. I wore a loose red dress, lacy tights, and black pumps. It wasn't nearly as tantalizing as my usual attire, but due to my slight weight gain, I was running out of clothes to wear. A small bump was beginning to form along my abdomen, making it impossible to fit into almost every item in my wardrobe. For now, I wanted to keep my pregnancy quiet. In order to do that, I had to wear clothes that would hide any sign of weight gain. Soon, I would have to buy maternity dresses, but not yet. Being heavily pregnant wouldn't do me any favors with the customers.

"That's a pretty name," he replied.

I smiled back. "Thank you. What's

yours?"

Since meeting Silas, I had never been intensely attracted to another man. But looking into those silky brown eyes, I felt my face grow red. Butterflies began to flutter in my stomach as my heart began to beat just a little bit faster.

"Eros," he answered.

I raised my eyebrows. "That's a weird name."

He laughed. "It's the name of the Greek god of love."

I blushed. "I know."

Eros leaned back in his chair. "Clever girl."

In an effort to distract myself, I began picking imaginary pieces of lint off my dress. He seemed to notice my discomfort but didn't look away. That only made me blush more. He was the type of man I hated to love. Eros had the perfect hair, body, and alluring grin. He was at least six-foot, and probably twice my weight. What a recipe for disaster.

"So, Delilah, what do you do when you're not at work?" he asked.

A few seconds passed before I was able to come up with a boring answer. "Oh, not much. What about you?"

He smiled, leaning forward. "Well, I enjoy taking pretty little women like you out."

I froze. "Is that so?"

In the back of my mind, I knew I shouldn't be flirting with him. It wasn't appropriate to entertain his advances, especially when Silas would probably be at my apartment when I arrived home. Eros did not need to be tangled up in my mess. Then again, Silas hadn't exactly been respectful toward me. The last time we were together, he'd slapped me and then pretended like nothing happened. Did I really owe him anything?

Eros was nice, and he seemed genuinely interested in me. He was actually trying to ask me out on a date rather than just commenting on my body. It was... thoughtful. I wanted to see where the conversation would lead.

"It is," he replied, taking another sip. "And I especially like it when they play hard to get. Makes the game so much more fun."

I twired a piece of my hair between my fingers. "Well, I suppose I'll have to see if you're a talented player."

He tilted his head back and chucked. "You're already entertaining me."

For a moment, a memory flashed before my eyes.

———

Silas leaned against the bar, light glimmering against his skin. It was dim in the room, but he seemed to shine despite the dark atmosphere. He brought a sense of energy everywhere he went. When I was with Silas, it felt like all of my senses were heightened. Suddenly, everything was more intense. The colors were brighter, the sounds were louder, and every flavor was magnified. He filled my life with vibrancy. Just being around him made me feel alive.

He glanced over, giving me a small wink. I blew him a kiss back. Silas stood guard casually, watching to make sure none of the other patrons tried to do anything stupid. He was by far the most intimidating man in the room. I knew he was watching me work, observing every swish of my hair and flutter of my eyelashes. He was territorial, more so than any other man I'd ever met. We'd only been dating for a few weeks at this point, but he was already hooked on me like a drug. We were both addicted to each other.

Silas walked over, leaned down, and

whispered in my ear. "We should get out of here."

I shook my head, giving him a knowing smile. "I have to work."

He groaned, stepping away. "Fine, I'll wait."

He stood there all night, simply watching me do my job and interact with customers. My tips weren't great that night, but I didn't really care. Having him be so concerned about me was electrifying. He viewed me as too valuable to let out of his sight for even a single moment, and that made me feel more powerful than anything else ever had.

———

"So," Eros said, "when can I take you out?"

My attention snapped back to the present. I wanted to accept his invitation, not only because he was my type but also because I was mad at Silas. Maybe this would make him realize I wasn't just a toy he could treat however he liked–I wasn't Athena. Silas needed to understand that I was the most beautiful woman he would ever be with and that he had to learn to respect me. I refused to let myself be hurt again, physically or mentally.

"Hmmm," I replied, "how about tonight?"

He raised his eyebrows. "When do you get off work?"

I glanced at the clock. "About an hour."

Eros grinned. "Then it's a date."

I worked for the next hour, refilling drinks and cleaning up abandoned glasses. Eros chatted casually with a few of the other customers, but I tried not to listen to their conversation. Just agreeing to go out with him made me nervous enough. After all, what would he think if I told him I was pregnant? I was trying to be careful about all the food and drink I consumed, as well as the activities I participated in. No, I wasn't reading any baby books, but I still took time to research the basics: no raw fish or large amounts of caffeine, etc.

Most men weren't enthusiastic about dating a pregnant woman, especially guys like Eros. He was good-looking, and on top of that, he had just the right combination of charisma and confidence to be incredibly dangerous. Playing with fire was rejuvenating, and it helped clear my mind of all the other topics I might rather not think of.

When the last customers finally left, Eros looked over at me. "It's probably not polite to ask, but...what happened to your face?"

I frowned. "You're right, that's a very rude question."

He nodded. "My curiosity overpowered my good manners, I'm sorry."

My face softened. "It's fine."

He paused. "It is…concerning, though."

I turned away from him. For some reason, I didn't want to lie to Eros. Maybe it was because he was being genuinely nice, or perhaps I just had an overwhelming need to receive approval from a particular type of man. Either way, I wanted to tell him the truth. Besides, I had never been one to keep quiet. "My boyfriend did it," I whispered.

He looked stunned. "You have a boyfriend."

I nodded. "Yes."

"And he…hit you?" Eros questioned.

"Yeah," I mumbled.

Eros rubbed his temple. "Wow, uh, not what I was expecting."

"What did you think I was going to

say?" I questioned.

He shrugged. "I don't know. Maybe you got into a fight with another girl or something."

I crossed my arms over my chest. "Well, if that had been the case, I would have won."

He roared with laughter, and I frowned.

"I have a feeling that's true," he replied.

I rolled my eyes. "It doesn't matter, anyway."

"I'm not sure about that," Eros said.

"Why?" I asked.

"When you agreed to go out with me, I assumed you were single," he said.

I frowned. "What does it matter to you?"

Eros sighed. "I'm not looking to start any drama. That's not what I need in my life. If you've got a man, I'm not going to interfere."

I paused. "Just a moment ago, you were concerned."

"And I still am," he replied, "but I'm not so invested that I'm going to pick a fight with some random guy I've never even met. You could just leave him and be done with it. After that, if he approached you again, I'd be more than happy to knock him out. I'll defend what's mine."

"Silas isn't the type of man you just walk away from," I answered.

Eros shook his head. "Then he's definitely not someone I want to make angry."

He stood from his chair and started walking toward the door. I was unable to find any words that might wound him as badly as he'd just hurt me. It wasn't that I wanted him to get involved with Silas or stand up for me, but it would have been nice to know he was willing to. A man had never been selfless for me like that before. And just once in my life, it would have been nice to see someone offer to protect me. That wouldn't happen, though, because I didn't deserve it. Maybe Eros could sense that. There was probably something in his gut telling him to run as far and fast away from me as possible. And honestly, that was the smartest thing to do."

Eros dropped fifty dollars on the counter before walking toward the door. "I'm sorry, Delilah."

And as I heard the door close behind him, I did nothing other than stare at the scrunched-up green paper he'd left as a peace offering.

Chapter Ten
EXPLANATION OR EXCUSE

A single black box sat in the bottom of my closet, untouched and covered in dust. I hadn't even thought about it for months. For the most part, I wasn't a sentimental person. In fact, I was quite the opposite. Never once had I hesitated to toss out my childhood artwork for perfect report cards. They meant nothing to me. But the contents of that black box…they were special.

With gentle hands, I reached down and lifted it into my arms. I retreated back to my bed, where I carefully removed the lid and began to examine the contents. Sitting on top were five pictures of me and my mother. They were the only thing I had to remind me of her. After her death, my father had discarded most of her belongings. He hadn't wanted to be reminded of her in any way, which was a hard thing to accomplish when I was in the picture. But somehow, these few photos survived.

I gingerly lifted them out of the box, closely examining each one. Over the years, I had probably looked at them a thousand times. Sometimes, weeks or months passed between when I pulled them out of the closet, and other times only days.

The first picture was taken when I was only a few days old. I'd been born with raven black hair, just like my mother and father. The stark contrast between my porcelain skin and otherwise bold, dark features had always seemed to fit my personality. But from everything I'd been told, my mother was different. According to the stories, she had been a soft woman. I remembered brief moments with her, but not enough to actually determine what she was like. Yet from those flashes of memory, I knew my mother had been nothing like me. While I was a monster, she had been loving and good.

I sometimes wondered if her death had impacted the person I'd grown to be. Maybe I would have been a better person if she was still alive. My father had taken care of me, but he was never an outwardly loving parent. I always had the material things I needed but not any sort of emotional connection. From a young age, I felt like I was on my own. I'd practically raised myself, acting like an adult even in my childhood years.

That wasn't a justification for the bad things I'd done. Maybe it was part of an explanation, though. Growing up without love had to hurt a child, right? No matter what anyone said, I knew it was the case. Or maybe it was just an excuse.

The rest of the pictures were from the weeks after I was born. In all of them, my mother looked like the most beautiful woman in the world. She was perfect in every way. That was at least a decent explanation of why my father had totally broken down after she died. It wasn't easy to handle losing someone you loved, especially when you had planned to spend your life together. Maybe my father resented me for reminding him of her. I'd probably never know for sure. After all, we didn't speak anymore.

I set the pictures aside, picking up the next item in the box. In my hands, I held a manilla envelope stuffed full of documents spanning over a decade. The first was from my first trip to a psychiatrist when I was just thirteen. I slid it out of the envelope, reading it again for what felt like the millionth time.

Though the document was about me, I was never supposed to receive it. After leaving the doctor's office, my father had hidden it from me. But what he hadn't known was that I'd overheard his conversation with the psychiatrist and knew exactly what it was about.

"I can't diagnose her so young, Mr. Banks," the doctor said.

My father frowned. "What is wrong with my daughter? I know there's something not right...something missing."

The doctor shook his head. "She's just a child, and it will be years before she fully develops. It would be unfair to give Delilah such a harsh diagnosis at her age. She's just a girl."

"Whatever it is, I need to know," my father replied.

The doctor sighed. "She shows many of the signs of Antisocial Personality Disorder."

My father frowned. "What does that mean?"

I continued to watch from behind the door as the doctor took a deep breath. "It's often associated with psychopathy, Mr.Banks."

The room fell silent. Although I didn't know what the condition was, I could tell it wasn't good. I didn't understand why my father had forced me to come here in the first place. Maybe it was because I just couldn't seem to make friends or because I was never able to control my anger. I fought him for months about the visit. He dragged me here anyway, though. All it had led to was bad news.

"She's a little girl. That's not possible," my father whispered.

"As I said, she's too young to be diagnosed," the doctor replied.

"But you're telling me you think that's the problem?"

The doctor nodded. "I'd gamble my salary

on it, Mr.Banks."

My father closed his eyes. "What do I do?"

There was another pause. "I wish I could tell you, Mr.Banks, I really do."

———

The paper I held in my hands was a copy of the doctor's notes from the many hours we'd spent together. In them, he detailed just how dangerous he thought I could become. Inside the envelope was the official diagnosis I'd received on my eighteenth birthday, along with the recommendations of a plethora of other doctors my father had demanded I see. They warned him of who I could become. And they were right about me being a monster. I had so many papers to prove just how little faith anyone had ever placed in me. All of their fears had eventually come to light. The only remaining question was if any of it was my fault, and I honestly wasn't sure. And yet still, in the back of my mind, I wondered if perhaps the doctor had made a mistake. If so, how had that impacted my perception of myself and the choices I'd made? I scrunched the papers into a tight ball and threw them across the room. There was nothing but evil inside me, and everyone knew it.

Chapter Eleven
THE REAL BIG BAD WOLF

I spent the next several weeks locked away in a dingy motel room. There wasn't much money in my bank account, so a small room with flickering lights and stains on the walls was all I could afford. It didn't matter much, though, because I spent most of my time sleeping. I lost track of how many calls from work I'd missed before finally turning off my phone. Silas had messaged me what felt like a million times, too. That's why I couldn't go back to my apartment. I'd made the mistake of giving him keys, but changing the locks would only make him more mad. Instead, I chose to hide.

In truth, I didn't have a plan for what

I was going to do. As the days ticked by, my pregnancy progressed further and further. I was tempted to end it all. If I died, too, I wouldn't feel as guilty about ending the baby's life. But whenever I tried my best to swallow a handful of pills, I always vomited them back up. My body refused to give in , no matter how hard I tried.

I often lay awake at night, wishing for a miscarriage. That would make my situation so much easier. It would eliminate any guilt I might otherwise feel while also allowing me to go back to my normal life. But there was a small part of my mind that knew my heart would break if I didn't keep the baby. For some reason, having this child meant a lot to me. Maybe it was just my hormones running wild.

I placed a hand on my stomach, imagining the tiny life tucked away inside me. What I had to decide was whether I was going to let Silas determine the course of my life. That wasn't something I really wanted to do, but I also refused to lose him. So, if I had to choose between the baby and the man I loved, which would I pick?

It didn't seem like a fair choice. Still, it was the situation I was in. Silas mattered more to me than anyone else ever had. If I could have him all to myself, that would be the key to finally being content. And that was all I wanted, really.

This pregnancy was…changing me. I didn't particularly like it. Feeling vulnerable made me uncomfortable. I wanted to feel strong again, to feel powerful. That didn't seem to be in the cards, though, at least not right now.

A knock sounded on the door, making me jump. Maybe it was the pizza I ordered. The baby was causing me to be hungry all day and night. This child was already annoying me, and he wasn't even born yet.

I slid out of bed, groaning as my achy body moved for the first time all day. As soon as I opened the door, my heart stopped beating. Silas was standing before me with a murderous expression on his face. There was violence in his eyes mixed with something like disdain. I took a slow step back, moving away from him as casually as possible.

"You've been avoiding me," Silas whispered.

His tone was deadly quiet, like the calm before a storm. I took a deep breath, trying to calm myself before replying. The last thing I needed to do was appear scared. That would only make him feel more dominant. Regardless of how badly I wanted to run and hide, I didn't have any other choice than to stand my ground. This was exactly the type of situation I'd been trying to avoid. It was too late, though. Silas had found me, and I could only imagine what kind of terrible punishment he had in mind. I was too tired to manipulate him. My hormones were driving me crazy, and the only thing I wanted to do was cry.

"I just needed to be by myself for a few days. I didn't mean to upset you," I replied in a soft, gentle voice.

"Too late," he growled.

I took another step back, bumping into the bedpost and losing my balance. Silas entered the room, slamming the door behind him. He clicked the lock into place before turning back toward me.

All I could think about was finding a way to run out the door without him grabbing me, but he was standing directly in my path. I'd never felt so much like prey before. Though I knew he did it to other women, I never thought he'd treat me this way.

In the back of my mind, the possibility of using my powers pressed upon me. I could easily stop all of this with just a flick of my wrist. He would be on his knees screaming in agony as lightning electrified every cell in his body. But for some reason, I just couldn't bring myself to do it. If I revealed the truth about who I was to Silas, he would run and never come back. That was something I couldn't live with. And so I was trapped, unable to protect myself even though it would have been almost effortless to do so.

"You haven't done it, have you," he said.

I shook my head. "Silas, don't do something you'll regret. Please, it's not worth it."

He snarled. "This is your fault. If you'd just cooperated, we wouldn't be in this situation."

"It's not your choice," I whispered, "it's mine."

He grabbed my arm, pulling my body against his. "You don't get to decide that. I'm not going to be tied down by this, Delilah. I have other things to worry about."

"You mean Athena?" I hissed.

"Shut. Your. Mouth," he whispered.

I pulled away, jerking my arm out of his grasp. "What is it about her? Why is she so special, Silas? I don't understand."

Silas lunged toward me, shoving me down onto the bed. "That's none of your business."

"It is!" I shouted. "I love you, Silas. You're supposed to love me, too."

He leaned over me. "If you actually felt that way, you would have done what I asked."

I tried to push him away, but he didn't move an inch. "I'm doing this because I love you! Can't you see that?"

He reached out, grabbing a handful of my hair and forcing my head back. "Why are you being so difficult? You're not even capable of love, Delilah. That emotion requires some speck of purity, and you have none."

Tears began to drip down my cheeks, and I despised myself for it. "Please...just, please."

Silas let go, and for a brief moment, I thought it was over. I closed my eyes, trying to stop the tears. Before I could open them again, something struck my abdomen. I screamed, reaching down as pain shot through my stomach. Silas was holding an expandable baton, the type of tool a woman might carry for self-defense. I cried out as he struck me again, attempting to reach out and stop him. My efforts were useless, though.

"Just give up, Delilah!" he shouted.

His expression was terrifying, but I couldn't bring myself to look away. Part of me wanted to beg him to stop, but I couldn't bring myself to do it. No matter what, I would not be weak. Silas would never gain that kind of control over me. I was better than that.

He leaned down to whisper in my ear. "If you just closed your eyes, this would be over quickly. Stop fighting it, and I won't hurt you more than necessary."

I stretched my fingers, desperately reaching for anything that would help me force him away. All I found was a pillow, but it would have to do. I threw it as hard as I could at his face. Silas laughed sadistically, swatting the pillow away. He seemed... amused by my attempt to protect myself. For a moment, I forgot the pain in my body and simply looked into his stormy eyes. There was something deranged about the man that even I couldn't fully comprehend. Maybe I wasn't the worst monster in the world. Perhaps in my attempts to find someone as equally evil as myself, I'd actually found a man far worse.

"Are you serious?" he whispered. "A pillow, Delilah? I thought you were smarter than that. Honestly, I'm surprised you don't have a stronger sense of self-preservation. You can't stop me, so just give in."

I pushed against his chest as hard as I could, but it didn't do a thing. Silas reached out and pinned my hands above my head. He squeezed my wrists so hard I thought they might break, but I didn't scream. That was the kind of satisfaction he wanted, and I wouldn't give it to him.

"What is wrong with you?" he growled.

I looked directly into his eyes. "Have

you ever wondered if maybe you're the problem?"

He rolled his eyes. "Really, Delilah, now is not the time for reflection."

For a moment, I thought I saw a flash of softness in his eyes. Before I could fully comprehend what that meant, it was gone. He leaned down again, brushing his lips against mine.

"If you go with me now, we can take care of the problem and forget this ever happened," he whispered.

I almost considered it. Maybe it was my hormones, or perhaps it was my refusal to ever let a man completely control my actions. Either way, I wouldn't let him win. His lips were only millimeters away from mine. I leaned up slowly, but he jerked away.

"Only if you agree," he said.

"Leave her," I whispered.

"What?" he replied.

"Leave Athena, and I'll get rid of the baby," I said.

He raised his eyebrows, almost as if he was actually considering the offer. "Why do you care so much about her?"

My heart slowed. "Because I don't want to share you. Is that so hard to understand? Why do you get to have both of us and yet we have to share you."

He rolled his eyes. "You're a woman, you wouldn't understand."

Tears began to flow from my eyes again. "How is it so complicated? I just want you."

Silas squeezed my wrists tighter, and I had to bite my lip not to scream. "It's natural, Delilah. You should just be satisfied with the time I give you and not ask for anything else. I provide for you, give you gifts, and make sure all your needs are met.

That's plenty."

He was being honest with me, and I hated it. Maybe I should have taken Ivan's offer. At least that way, I would have been safe. He probably would have given me a little freedom, too. Not to mention that he wasn't violent. Silas was every bad thing wrapped up in one irresistible package. But no matter how logical it would have been, I couldn't force myself to walk away.

"It's not though, Silas, it's not," I whispered.

There was a brief pause where we simply stared at each other. While I wanted it to be true, I knew there was no way he was actually reconsidering anything. Silas had made up his mind, and he wasn't the type of man who could be easily persuaded to admit he was wrong. Maybe I had overestimated how much I meant to him. Was I just another plaything?

He pulled away, once again reaching for the baton. "You made your choice, and now we both have to live with it."

I tried to move, but pain once again clouded my mind. It then occurred to me exactly what he was trying to do. Silas was going to kill his own child and maybe me in the process. And the worst part was he viewed it as my doing. I had no doubt he blamed me for getting pregnant in the first place, even though it was certainly his fault. This had never been part of my plan. As he struck me again, I couldn't imagine a more evil act than beating the pregnant mother of your child to death. There was something uniquely sick about trying to kill your own flesh and blood. I could only hope that he didn't truly contemplate what he was doing. Because if he did, well, I had managed to find the worst man on the planet to give my soul to.

Maybe I deserved all the pain and suffering. That was entirely possible. And perhaps if it was just me, I wouldn't have been opposed to him beating me until I couldn't breathe. But the baby inside me had done nothing wrong. He had never chosen to be created. And it certainly wasn't my child's fault that his father hated him. I couldn't believe I had ever been stupid enough to think having his baby would make Silas promise to leave all other women behind. That's what a good man would have done. And if I had chosen a decent partner, that might have been my fate. Either way, my child did not deserve to suffer because of my bad decisions.

I kicked my legs out, pushing Silas away as hard as I could. He shouted in surprise, stumbled back a step before regaining his balance. I sat up, ignoring the pain in my abdomen as I raced for the door. My hand was reaching for the lock when I felt him tug on my dress, dragging me down. The next thing I knew, the world went black.

Chapter Twelve
LOVE IS...

When I woke, the smell of blood was everywhere. It took me a few moments to realize I was lying on the dirty motel carpet with an open wound on the back of my head. Although it took me a few moments, I eventually managed to force my body up into a sitting position. That's when I noticed the crimson liquid covering the otherwise tan-colored floor. I was lying in a puddle of blood, and the sight of it made my head spin. My clothing was soaked as well. It was hard to believe I could lose so much blood without dying.

"Good, you're awake," Silas said.

My head snapped up at the sound of

his voice. Silas was lying on the bed wearing nothing other than a pair of loose-fitting jeans. He leaned back against the headboard, sipping on a glass of amber liquid.

"I was starting to worry you might be dead," he remarked.

I looked down at my body, wondering how exactly I was still breathing. He must have beat me even more after I passed out. I winced at the thought of my limp body being broken into pieces while I was totally unaware.

Silas tossed a washcloth on the floor beside me. "Here, I got this out of the bathroom for you."

I picked it up, wondering how he thought the tiny piece of fabric would be able to clean the terrifying amount of blood off my body and the floor. My head was spinning, and I had a hard time focusing my vision. It was entirely possible that I was still bleeding internally. Maybe I was going to die and just didn't know it yet.

"I'm glad I don't have to dispose of your body," Silas mused. "That would have been a shame. You're just too pretty for that. But a man has to do what he has to do. It's always difficult with you women."

I slowly lifted my dress just enough to see exactly how much damage had been done. When I saw the clump of remains, I almost vomited. It looked as if it had been pounded to death, which is exactly what had happened. My stomach and thighs were covered in purple bruises that went all the way up to my ribs.

"It's not pretty, but you'll heal," Silas said, his voice slightly gentler.

I looked at him, furry in my eyes. "How could you?"

"It didn't have to be this way, Delilah," he whispered.

My hands were now covered in dried blood, and my body began to shake. Silas stood from the bed, reached down, and pulled me up into his arms. I let him carry me like a ragdoll. Silas set me softly down atop the covers before wiping the hair out of my face.

"Such a shame," he whispered.

I closed my eyes, trying to ignore the rising nausea. "What?"

"I was going to spend the night, but I don't think I can while you're in this... condition," he replied.

I looked up at him. "Where are you going?"

He tilted his head to the side, then reached down to stroke my cheek with his finger. "Where do you think?"

A sob escaped my throat. "Please... don't go to her."

He shrugged. "I'll be back tomorrow.

In the meantime, clean yourself. And maybe call housekeeping. It looks like someone was murdered here."

I had to stop myself from saying that that was exactly what had happened. Silas ran a hand through his hair, and once again, I was struck by how undeniably gorgeous he was. No matter how evil his actions were, it didn't take away from the fact that he was by far the most beautiful man I'd ever met.

Silas turned around and began walking toward the door. But before he touched the lock, he looked back around at me. His eyes skimmed my body, and I couldn't even bear to imagine what he was thinking about.

"I do love you, Delilah," he whispered.

And with that, he left the room and closed the door behind him.

Chapter Thirteen
FEAR

The next morning was even worse. Slowly, I managed to make my way to the bathroom. Though every muscle in my body ached, I forced myself to wash the dried blood off my skin. I was numb to everything. Yesterday's events almost didn't seem real. It was like a terrible nightmare I just couldn't wake up from.

I had always known Silas was a bad person. He had never seemed like a knight in shining armor to me, but I was okay with that. And yet, I had been under the impression that there were certain levels of evil he wouldn't sink to. After all, even criminals had their own moral code. But

Silas, I wasn't sure he had any sense of right or wrong outside of what benefited him. Sure, I wasn't a righteous person either. But I had vowed to never hurt that baby. Now, it didn't even matter. The child was gone.

I'd been clueless about what to do with the remains. There didn't seem to be any right answer. All I knew was that I didn't want to elongate the process more than necessary. Ultimately, I decided to simply flush the toilet. And honestly, I kind of hated myself for it. The whole thing felt so wrong. It was the only solution I could come up with on my own, especially since I wasn't going to receive help from anyone.

After scrubbing my skin raw, I finally stepped out of the shower. There was nothing else to do except leave the motel. I would just go back to my normal life, or at least try to. The main question was if I could forgive Silas for what he had done.

I knew he didn't deserve it. He was abusive and unrepentant. Most women would have probably called the police. That would have been the smartest thing to do. After all, he could have killed me. I had no clue what other internal injuries I might have, though I suspected I probably had some sort of concussion. My whole body was covered in bruises, and I doubted it would start healing for days, maybe even weeks.

Being a faerie didn't give me any sort of supernatural healing powers. That was the main thing I envied about the fictional fae. Some of them were more like superheroes than our actual species. We didn't live for hundreds of years or have courts in other realms. No, we were stuck in the mortal world just like everyone else. However, if I could have chosen one ability possessed by those fictional beings, it would be the power to mend myself faster than any doctor. It would have been convenient, especially in this situation.

I briefly wondered if I should perhaps just leave Silas. Maybe that was the right course of action. I could just block him, move to a different state, and forget about this whole nightmare. But that would have meant giving in, and I wasn't the type of person to let my decisions be influenced by others. I normally didn't care what sorts of names people called me. They could say I was the devil-incarnate, and it wouldn't matter. But I refused to be viewed as weak. That was something I would not tolerate. They could call me malicious, manipulative, and narcissistic. In truth, maybe those things were true. But I would not let anyone say I was a coward, especially Silas. No man was allowed to speak about me like that.

After last night, I wasn't sure if I loved

him or not. Maybe I was just obsessed. It didn't matter, though. After how hard I'd fought for him, I wasn't going to let Athena steal Silas away from me so easily.

I put a pair of Victoria's Secret sweatpants on before pulling a matching sweatshirt over my head. In normal circumstances, I never would have worn an outfit like this outside my house. But today was different. For the next twenty-four hours, I would allow myself to be sad. I would feel all of the emotions so that when the sun rose tomorrow, I didn't have to feel sorry for myself anymore. One day of self-pity was enough. Any more than that would make me start to lose my edge. I pulled my hair back into a ponytail and applied a minimal amount of makeup. No matter how badly I felt, I'd never go outside without concealer and mascara. That had been the case since I was in high school, and it definitely wasn't going to change now.

I jumped when my phone started ringing. There was no one I wanted to talk to, but out of habit, I answered anyway. There was an unfamiliar voice on the other end of the line.

"Hello?" I said.

"Is this Delilah Banks?" the woman replied.

There was no caller ID, and I didn't have the slightest idea where the stranger was from. Part of me was tempted to just hang up, but curiosity prevented me from doing so. My day couldn't get any worse, right?

"Yes," I answered.

"I have your bloodwork results," she said. "You're having a little girl. Congratulations!"

My phone clattered to the ground. The world was frozen still. It was all I could do to keep breathing. I dropped to my knees, my head falling between my hands. Suddenly, it was all so, so real. Before, it was almost as if I could pretend none of it had happened. If no one else mentioned the baby, I might have been able to move past it as if the whole thing had been an illusion. And not knowing the gender that had made the fetus seem like a living being. But now, all I could picture was a little girl who looked exactly like Silas, with a shining smile and sparkling eyes. This was what heartbreak felt like. My chest was so full of pain I thought it might tear open.

All of a sudden, a scream erupted from my mouth. It was like I was no longer in control of my own body. My skin and bones felt foreign, as if they belonged to a stranger. Rage, grief, and regret coursed through me. All I wanted was to burn the world down for her, for the baby that never had a chance to live, love, and be happy.

I seemed to watch from afar as the stranger who inhabited my body grabbed the bedside table and threw it against the ground. The action was only a brief relief. I needed more destruction. Nothing other than violence could distract me from the unending anger that had overtaken my soul. I couldn't live with this, not when I felt the guilt of it weighing me down.

The next few hours were a blur. I tore the sheets and pillows to shreds like a wild animal. Glass from the lamp and picture frames ended up all over the floor, cutting into my feet and making me bleed. Both bed frames were broken and scattered about the room. Eventually, I collapsed on the floor, exhaustion overpowering any extra will I had to keep going. Tears poured down my cheeks, but I wasn't sure if they were from grief, anger, or both. It didn't matter.

The tears slowed to a soft drip and finally stopped flowing. My eyes began to flutter shut as the room seemed to fade away into darkness. I could feel all the broken glass stuck in my feet and under my body, but the physical pain was at least a distraction from what I felt on the inside. And in that moment I wondered if perhaps I really was a coward, because if I'd just had a little more courage, I would have ended it all.

Epilogue

When I opened my eyes again, ten hours had passed. It was the middle of the night. There was nothing other than total silence and complete destruction surrounding me. In the most secretive part of my heart, I had hoped someone would discover me. Maybe that's why I'd caused such a mess. Never before had I been able to ask for help, and I certainly wasn't going to start now. Besides, there was no one who cared about me enough to bother checking if I was dead or alive. The workers at this dingy motel weren't bothered as long as they kept charging my credit card, and the other patrons were too busy with their own problems to bother calling the police. If I had died in that room, no one would have discovered me until the smell became so bad that someone finally complained.

Silas hadn't come back. I should have predicted that he wouldn't. He was waiting for me to fall onto my knees in front of him and beg for forgiveness. It made me sick that he actually expected me to be that weak. I was better than that, or at least I thought so. Silas would not get that much of a victory over me.

I hated him more than I'd ever despised anyone in my life. Well, maybe, except Athena. If it weren't for her, none of this would have happened. She was the reason Silas had refused to accept my pregnancy. I didn't understand why, but he viewed her as too valuable to lose. And for no other reason, I wanted her dead. She would pay for this. The best part was that hurting her would pain Silas more than if I stabbed him to death. It would not only make him lose his precious little dove but also embarrass him because he couldn't protect her. It was the perfect way to kill two birds with one stone.

I would get my revenge, no matter how long it took. If I had to spend months or years waiting for the perfect time to strike, that's what I would do. I was more than capable of evil deeds; I'd done them several times before. This was even more personal, though. For the first time, I was angry because someone I loved had been harmed. Even though I never got to hold, kiss, or love my baby, I was angry for her. Somehow, I would make Athena suffer just as much as I had. This would not be the end of my story.

The End

To see what happens next, read Fallen Snow, the third book in the EverGreen Trilogy.

Abby Farnsworth is the YA paranormal and urban fantasy romance author of the EverGreen Trilogy. Her books are targeted toward teens and young adults but can be enjoyed by readers of all ages.

She enjoys traveling, history, and reading a good book. When not working on her next novel, she can be found taking long walks exploring the natural world, trying a new recipe, or singing in various ensembles.

She currently resides in West Virginia with her family but adores trips to the beach, mountains, cities, and historical landmarks.

To learn more about Abby, her books, and current projects, take a look at the following:
#authorabbyfarnsworth
#theevergreentrilogy